good deed rain

Books by Allen Frost

Ohio Trio
Bowl of Water
Another Life
Home Recordings
The Mermaid Translation
The Selected Correspondence of Kenneth Patchen
The Wonderful Stupid Man
Saint Lemonade
Playground
Roosevelt
5 Novels
The Sylvan Moore Show
Town in a Cloud
A Flutter of Birds Passing Through Heaven:
    A Tribute to Robert Sund
At the Edge of America
Lake Erie Submarine
The Book of Ticks
I Can Only Imagine
The Orphanage of Abandoned Teenagers
Different Planet
Go with the Flow: A Tribute to Clyde Sanborn
Homeless Sutra
The Lake Walker
A Hundred Dreams Ago
Almost Animals
The Robotic Age
Kennedy
Fable
Elbows & Knees: Essays & Plays
The Last Paper Stars
Walt Amherst Is Awake
When You Smile You Let in Light

WHEN YOU SMILE YOU LET IN LIGHT

Allen Frost

When You Smile You Let in Light © 2019
Allen Frost, Good Deed Rain
Bellingham, Washington
ISBN 978-1-64516-990-1

Writing: Allen Frost
Cover Illustrations: Casper Truong
     also: Eye, Flower, Girl
City Illustration: Daniel Jones
Cover Production: Jen Armitage
Journal Illustrations: Allen Frost, 1989
Apple: TFK!

*What consideration and tenderness I could show
her! If it were a movie, I would have only to wait.
The bus would get lost or the city would be bombed
and she and I would tend the wounded.*

—Walker Percy, *The Moviegoer*

WHEN YOU SMILE YOU LET IN LIGHT

INTRODUCTION

This is the second book I wrote. It started in college, with trips to Boston for inspiration, riding the Red Line and raining winter nights. This adventure follows in the footsteps of my first novel, *Blue Anthem Wailing* (to be published soon!) with more time travel through a rough America. The manuscript went through a few different drafts. The journal I kept in New York City was one of the sources. I loved the American Museum of Natural History and I actually had a way of getting in for free.

During that time I was also writing *Bagdad Butterfly of Panama* (published in *At the Edge of America*, 2016). Both books feature that museum. I had a favorite old movie theater too and I got to see Charlie Chan, W.C. Fields and Mae West like it was 1942. I went to that big publisher's tower at Rockefeller Center with a manuscript tucked under my arm. This book evolved as I moved around and experienced different worlds. At one point, Harriet was running for political office. And Glass' name started as Look Up. I don't know where Glass Benedict Arnold came from. For a while, the manuscript was called *Steamtime, Mother of Exiles* but the final title came from a dream. I love discovering books in dreams. Anytime that happens, I try my best to write down what I find.

--AF
January 2019

falling

He had been watching the corner for days, where the flowers ran into the street. A shop selling long stem colors in the rain, under all the neon lights and office windows. Somewhere a day was waiting for him like a prayer.

In all the falling down Glass Benedict Arnold had been doing, in all of his imagining of the end of the world, he was surprised by this sunny afternoon. On a bright blue day like this, he was afraid of the apocalypse.

Leaving the movie theater, poured from that black and white silent world, he tried to fit himself back. He leaned into his shadow drawn on the pavement, moving faster underfoot.

A rocket roar rattled the buildings while he was trying to accustom his senses back to colors.

Crossing the street, he glanced to his sides

and there was the end of the world. Framed between two black buildings torn into the blue sky, a white contrail was curling over. He froze between the lines of the crosswalk as the sound shot through the city. Panic frozen for seconds, he didn't know whether to run, seek shelter, or just stand there and watch the last seconds of life.

A missile traveling a thousand miles per hour and carrying megatons of explosives is not something you can outrun, he knew—the fearealization that mankind is going to destroy itself, trying to take everything else with it. Suddenly the time had come for America to vanish—the end—America was gone.

The contrail hung in the sky for an icy moment, cold as a black spider dangling from a web, pausing in lowering itself down for the kill…and then the smoke curved away, back up into the air. An airplane, not the end of the world, just an acrobat overhead.

Jets screamed figure-eights through the sky-scrapers, tearing smoke trails across the sky. He wanted to run like someone on fire.

A crowd of people at the curb smiling, jabbing each other, pointing at the performance saw the Blue Angels flying over the city.

Flashing low above the city, and past the windows of all the tall offices, people stood watching, pointing and following. Just the opposite of Glass, they didn't see what he saw, or feel what he felt. They had no idea what he knew.

Over the walls his shadow traveled, across the spray-painting and charred bricks. A geometric shape went overhead while he looked down at the bones of Indians stacked below street level.

"Hello, this is Lenina…I don't want to sound…to be…It's probably nothing." She tried not to cry into the phone. In times like this, her softly hidden Georgia accent would knead into her sentences forming her words like wet clay. "I don't know about things anymore…I don't think I belong here. I know mom and dad said we had to be strong, but I don't know if I can."

Sometimes it made her cry and she would lose her hope; it would fly from her and circle around her. She couldn't find it again unless someone caught it for her and returned it to her. Her sister helped and Lenina listened to her voice until she could calm down again. She could remember to smile and she would change. She laughed at her sister's words and continued, "Yesterday it just came over me. I was crying and I grabbed a cab to get out of there. I must have looked like a disaster. Do you ever feel that as people get older, they forget how to—hey, is that Louis?" She heard the trumpet in the background of her sister's apartment. "No! Leave it, I love Louis Armstrong. It reminds me of the days we used to be together. Mmhmmm. You know the cab driver—that's what I wanted to tell you—I was crying like a fish when I got in the cab and I gave my address and I just wanted to get home and it was like a movie you'd see. The driver looked exactly like Herbie Hancock."

She switched the phone to her other ear. "Yes, and there was jazz playing in the cab and we talked and when he stopped he said he wanted me not to worry. He smiled and said everything was going to be alright."

Then her eyebrows knit, "What sound?" Lenina removed the phone from her ear to listen. "Oh, it's those carolers again!"

She looked at the closed door of her apartment.

"Come all ye faithful!" she sang back to the door. The caroling moved onward like a ship through the building.

Lenina laughed and asked, "You can hear them?" She laughed again, "I know. For weeks they keep coming back to the apartments. Someone must be feeding them." She smiled as she listened to her sister, "I know!" She laughed and explained, "They're bringing tidings of comfort and joy, comfort and joy," she sang with a laugh. She wiped her hand over her eyes.

"Yes…I've been getting ready for the performance." She looked down at her fingers, made a violin motion. "Slowly but surely…It'll be alright, I suppose…I hope you don't mind that I called. I didn't mean to start crying on your shoulder. I'm sorry about all this. I feel a lot better now though. I just had to talk to someone."

Now these are like things seen in copper.

A Pearl Harbor morning, smoky fires charring the blue sky. Knocked out of flight by an ambulance, a bird flaps on the road. Its small brown wings tick a small desperate pinwheel. After it stops beating, the bird rests on its side, one foot pointing claws at the sky. The black eyes watch. With another flurry, the bird skitters closer to the green edge of the road.

The bay is still burning with the sinking warships.

Feathers and the clipped wings broken hopelessly, swimming circles on the tar. The bird tries to shake itself over to the sand, off the paving. More sirens and car tires miss it. Like a toy that ran out of winding, it gave one more flap. The beak panted.

Water is filling the drowning ships. The wind is burning. The sea is chopping with boats. Gulls fly out of the dark clouds.

Their family history began with this fire that herded a girl to a concentration camp and finally flowed like water into Glass. They were all a part of America that began here. Nature's time will cover that war with rust and build coral tombs hiding over the bulk of sunken battleships, making something for colored fish out of the loss. Waves wash away and floating in the air overhead, another bird appears.

Rolling along the clicking tracks, Glass slouched in the subway car. He looked out the black window at the dark underground tunnel. Sometimes it streaked with the green-yellow flash of another passing train. He wasn't thinking of anything, he was done with work for the day. His mind was wandering.

The door between cars opened and slammed shut as The Magnificent Marvelous Magic Man appeared. Going from car to car towards the front of the train, he announced himself, asking for money, working his way through the doors. Glass had seen him perform a few times before.

"I'm The Magnificent Marvelous Magic Man. I can play every instrument in the world, but I choose a comb and this piece of torn newspaper." He played the "Hawaii 5-0" theme twice and the riders gave him a dollar in coins. His paper cup rattled like a tambourine.

Glass pretended it was the greatest show on Earth.

Someone had written in pen on his plastic seat, smudged, "The world is over in 1986" and he wondered why it was still here.

When the door slid open at the last stop, hot air escaped, hot air entered, along with the people departing and arriving. He stared out the window and saw his mother's ghost.

There she was, leaning up against the green tiled pillar, looking over at him with a kind of smile. The rap on someone's radio played through the open door. Everyone knew the new Public Enemy. A man with a newspaper folded the headlines, "U.S And South Africa Trade" under an arm. People swept around his mother like wind. All of them moved, until the train closed its doors and lurched back down the tunnel into dark.

He wondered if she would be at the next station too. He needed her. In the middle of all this madness and trying to figure things out, he really needed her. He needed her to be around him all the time, or at least never too far away.

But she didn't reappear and the ride back was more alone, listening to the monotonous clapping rails, until the doors finally sighed open at his stop. His empty footsteps walked the dark neighborhoods to the house and up to his room.

The sound of the radio music faintly lulled from down the hall.

Glass had gone in quietly so he wouldn't wake Harriet or her daughter. He had stepped carefully up the restless creaking wooden stairs to his room and he sat down on his bed.

He put a record on and it spun him towards the ghost's arrival.

"Glass," she whispered in his ear. She was close enough to feel the warmth of her breath across his neck. He turned and saw her ghost sitting on the bed with him.

Her legs were folded under her, blue dress, her long dark brown hair, smiling despite the cutting distance of time and death. She hugged him. She felt half real. When he opened his eyes, staring along her neck, he noticed she wore the colored wooden bead necklace he made for her in kindergarten.

"How are you?" she asked.

He sighed truthfully. Her eyes were half in

ghostland.

"You'll feel better when you have something to believe in," she told him.

A wave went over her and she looked like a watery ghost. "I'm sorry it had to happen. I'm just glad I can still return to be with you some-times."

When she vanished he got up and went to his bookshelf. He found a familiar, friendly old book. Opening its frayed red covers, a photo-graph fell out into his palm. It was a picture of his mother. She was wearing that necklace he just saw on her. That was how he remembered her now. He slid the picture back between the pages and replaced the book. Memories of a photo.

After he left his room, he quietly shut his door, left the house the way it was. Back out-side, he headed for the station again. He carried a tape recording of Charlie Parker and Dizzy Gillespie.

A light rain outside fell from the black sky. The shoulders of his coat were dotted with little spots. Walking to the subway, he could see in-side the windows of the street level apartments. In one living room he saw a blue TV screen showing pictures of a sinking warship and a waving American flag.

The train was waiting at the station when Glass got there. Sometimes he was lucky. He found an orange plastic seat. Hot yellow lights. A man opposite him read a newspaper. "Navy Ship Hit By Missile." The bored train hummed and waited for the time to move.

With a whistle, the doors rolled shut and the train wheels spun. Shadowy buildings walked by. Beads of dew ran down the windows. The night had rained itself out, but the streets still splashed the lights of the city.

Glass was about to put the headphones on and listen to "Ornithology" when the train stopped. Like a cow in a wet field of dandelions, it stopped and decided to stay put.

The man across from him was reading another page, "Navy Vows Revenge." Glass could tell he was pretending not to care, but he could see him glancing at the window nervously.

When the door hissed open, a man in the gray train uniform stepped inside to announce, "I'm sorry folks, you'll have to switch trains."

The sound of a newspaper being folded,

"Navy Ship H—" People leaving the train, some were outside already.

Glass stood up. He could feel the cool air. Green lit streets, blinking red and white car lights, black and blue silhouette people huddled near the track and feeling just like him, "Where am I?"

A kid was singing in a squeaky voice, "My country tis of me" down in the darkened shadowed nowhere. Standing in a cold breeze, not caring. The tracks led on past figures filing darkly into the city ahead,

"You'll have to switch trains to the opposite side," said the man in uniform. He pointed from their broken train to another one.

Along the tracks, Glass noticed the people holding signs that read, "On Strike!" They walked back and forth numbly, wearing windbreakers and sweaters. Someone down the line yelled, "We demand equal opportunities, equal pay!"

The next train had more people in it. Across from Glass a woman played with a baby and someone awkwardly tall reading a comic book aloud, "Oh I forgot, you control the mood I'm in. I remember that..." The comic book world continued while tall green patriotic statues rolled past the windows and two people were still arguing over an empty seat.

The museum was closed. All the lights were off. Glass got in by using his own key and he knew his way through the dark, up the stairs and down the hall. Animals looked awake in their displays, frozen, but they were always listening. The museum was filled with them.

They reminded him of the fireflies he kept in a jar. They danced like static in the glass by his bed. A glow of candle in his mother's hair and smoothed across her cheek like that buttercup trick. If you rub the flower under your chin and if the petals reflect on your skin, you must like butter. Singing songs and bedtime stories. Nighttime purples all around him and the blue of outside peeks in through the window curtains. Car tires splash on the street. And he also hears the rubbing calls of moon wet crickets off in the dark field behind the house, enjoying the summer night in their tall weeds. When his mother sighs and sings above his sleepy six year old head, the lullabies carry him. There is a train that runs at night, back away on the distant horizon of the dozing-off-boy-meets-sleep-neighborhood, chugging and whistling and wishing goodnight with its many spinning metal wheels.

A sleek looking ghostly gray bird watched him approach.

Glass pointed, "Hello Passenger Pigeon." This was a bird that understood him. He turned on the tape recorder and the bird listened to the music and listened to him when he spoke. "Nature is supposed to know what it's doing. There may be strange mistakes, but in the end everything has its place, doesn't it? So why'd we turn out this way? Has it to do with what they scream on street corners? Were we really cast out of some Eden? Nature didn't want us to belong? Are we really that wrong?"

The Passenger Pigeon in its clear display case watched him quietly.

"Shouldn't there be a future for everyone? Maybe soon I'll be doomed just like you in there."

He sighed and listened to the music and tried to think.

Harriet. Harriet was someone he could open to.

Harriet knew he was more than meets the

eye. Harriet was the only one who knew about these midnight forays to play music to the animal statues. When she laughed, her smile was the joy of being alive. As they walked through the park, sweet smell of fall and colored leaves hanging on trees like bright candy, Harriet said, "I guess it makes sense that passenger pigeons would like jazz." Harriet even asked if she could meet him there sometime.

Harriet.

The passenger pigeon was deep in concentration, brooding on piano, trumpet, saxophone, so Glass decided to give Harriet a call. There was a phone down the hall, not far from the white stuffed mountain goats.

The phone had a typed list of employee's names next to it. The edges were torn and some numbers were crossed out and rewritten in pen. Like animals, people migrated. Glass and Harriet shared the same number. After dialing, the pause before the ringing was filled in by Charlie Parker. The phone rang three times and then there came an answer.

Like the creak of a rusted red wagon wheel, her voice, warm as a cat comforting purr in her bed, a dreamy tired, "Hello?"

"Harriet, this is Glass."

And then her voice took on shape, like the snap crackle before a record and then the suddenness of sound as someone starts to sing: "Glass! Where are you? Oh, you're at the museum, aren't you?" He could picture the concern in her dark blue eyes.

He felt sorry that he called her. He wished he hadn't woken her, but he suddenly missed her not being near. He apologized.

"No, no," she said, "Don't worry. Rachel just came to my room. She had a bad dream and now she wants to go on a fieldtrip. Would you like to go to the museum and see Glass?" she asked her daughter. He heard the little girl sing and Harriet laughed and told him, "We'll come over, that would be fun. The night is young." She turned on the bedside lamp. The bright glow made her squint, blink and look away. She scratched her hair and the shadows in her hand. She looked at the clock. "We'll be there soon."

His head spinning, now happy.

"Yes, I'll see you soon!" Rachel called.

They hung up their phones.

Harriet flopped her legs out of bed, and the cool air climate made her bare skin tingle. She started to pull on her clothes, cold jeans and shirt and sweater lying on the floor where she had dropped them earlier. She yawned at the clock, "Glass..." He was always her worry.

And he walked back to the display case. He stared at the pigeon in there. Another lonely soul. He was glad they would be over soon.

He was so tired when he sat down with his back to the bird, he could easily see himself falling asleep. While the ghost fluttered around the bones of extinct creatures sleeping in the dark.

"It's amazing there are still spirits in this age," he lazily told the Passenger Pigeon. His mother was on her way, walking through walls and crowds to be with him and he remembered the first time he saw her ghost.

On the playground at school, "Your mother…" the principal was talking to him. "There's been an accident. Your mother's in the hospital." Glass dropped from the monkey bars. "No she's not," pointing, "She's right over there." His mother held the other end of a skipping rope.

He knew he had been dreaming when he woke to music and a pair of footsteps. Standing up as she came into the gloom, he rubbed his eyes.

They walked in like Christmas. "Good morning!" Harriet's hair was rumbled by windy sleep and she held a jar of orange juice and bread. She took off her big wool brown coat. "It's freezing outside!" She stamped, rubbing her hands and she laughed aloud, "Look at you! Asleep with the dinosaurs!"

The shadow of a brontosaurus stretched down the hall towards them.

Rachel danced around them and Glass smiled.

Harriet took him to live in her home as her own son after his mother died. It wasn't easy, but he discovered love because of her. He used to dream and really wish for someone just like her to appear.

Harriet smiled, "I figured you must be hungry. I even have some jam and butter for the bread, which you'll be glad to know I heated up in the oven before I came over. It's barely warm now though. Let's eat it before it cools anymore." Setting the food down on her spread out coat, she cut slices of bread for them. "Aren't you hungry?"

He found himself just standing there, watching her. She was kneeling on her coat, pressing out a section for him to join her, holding out the piece of bread. Rachel sat down like a duck next to her mother and took the bread from her hand.

"Rachel!"

"Sorry," Rachel mumbled.

"Would you like to offer Glass the next piece?"

Her daughter nodded and Harriet kissed her. "That would be nice." She began cutting the bread. "How are things at the museum tonight? I see you've got the myna bird all excited."

The one alive bird, the museum pet, was fluttering from branch to branch, with the music playing.

"She's happy to see you," Glass said.

"Mmm." Harriet bit into the bread, oranged over with marmalade. "Hey, this is good!"

Glass agreed. "A picnic at the museum." It sounded like a Charlie Chaplin movie.

"Oh! I forgot to tell you. I won't be coming into work tomorrow. Rachel and I are going to the country. One of her friends is having a birthday party at her farm." She took a drink and said, "You should come with us, you know. Call in sick!" Her eyes glittered. "They have a lake and goats and sheep and of course Rachel wants to bring her butterfly net."

He saw how it would be—Harriet's daughter running down the wind, trying to catch winter butterflies.

"It's supposed to be sunny and warm tomorrow," Harriet glowed. "If we can believe the newspaper."

He imagined her gambling a handful of clouds for a sunny day.

"But even if it's not that warm it will still be fun. Would you like to come with us?"

"I don't know," Glass said slowly.

"I think you should." Her face became serious then her words started to come down like crow feathers. "Glass, you've got to let yourself see the outside world. Like this dark place you're in right now. Nothing good can happen if you don't open up and let light in."

He knew that. He knew she was right, but oh how he was always hoping that ghost would show up and take him away.

She was like a wasp walking on window glass, around and around. She kept a hand on her belly as she carried her sign over her shoulder, around and around. She thought about her child that was going to be born into this self-destruction. She even wondered out loud, "Is it all going to end?" and she even worried at the worst, "What am I doing bringing a baby into this world?" Her thoughts and cares bounced around in her. "It's an unsafe world for babies. For Everyone. It seems nobody likes anybody in America…What's wrong? We're burning up our children like kindling. We're at war and we're in the middle of a revolution and the whole thing is ready to ignite with a nuclear torch."

The safety soft round of her belly was creating Glass anyway. She held a hand over the universe.

She did everything she could to end the war for the good of the country, but also personally. Glass's father was somewhere in that Vietnam blowing up on TV.

Not even having a child could stop his going.

Once he was gone, she knew he would never come back. Did he know too? Bombs for

Christmas in Hanoi. The keepers of war weren't letting go. The crashing of it all could be heard everywhere. Signs and fists. Police and uniforms. Guns and clubs. Trying to make a better society seemed suicidal. And all the while, she was still thinking of her growing baby, knowing this wasn't the end, it was just a new beginning.

Finally it came to her so simply: life was reason enough.

So she created him like a poem.

international harvester

The alarm clock rang. Fog filled the street below, moving lightly, fumbling its smoky way through the gray neighborhood. It made the windows and metal rails wet, leaving beads of water. His bedroom curtains sighed open, and he saw the morning crawling in. Harriet and he would leave soon for the trip to the country.

A car moving on the road, Glass in the front seat next to Harriet and the talking, singing of children in stereo behind him in the backseat.

Industrial graveyards lined the way out of the city. Fences locked round the factories had turned them into cemeteries. Past shut down mills with broken windows. Pigeons in the burned out cars next to railroad tracks. Too many chimneys have gone into making the city, standing like petrified forests. Their car left town like a mechanical carpet of land was pulled out from underneath.

"You'll have a great time," she was telling

Glass. Her hand poked out of its blue parka sleeve to tap the windshield wipers on. The metal arms streaked the glass clear. "The weather isn't as good as it was supposed to be, but that figures, doesn't it?" She let some trees fly by. "It feels so nice to be getting out of the city though."

Slowly the green took over from cement.

He turned around. The kids twisting on the backseat were fogging up the windows with their breath and drawing pictures on the glass. Rachel drew butterfly shapes with her fingertip.

They drove by bulldozers clawing the ground, paving the way for another shopping mall, waiting to spring concrete flowers. The world was in danger. When nature itself is no bigger than a spider, it survives however it can. He remembered a nightmare. Somehow the sky was being torn up and graded away. Whenever a dream got too bad, he would wake up. He opened his eyes and the sound was machines outside his window plowing the snow off the streets. Blinking orange and red lights reflected up onto his ceiling through the shades. That was years ago, when Harriet had to hold his hand back into sleep.

The gray shell of a nuclear power plant

shuddered by and the trees growing near it must be warning us, he thought, to stay away.

I don't know why the heat doesn't work in this car," Harriet said. "It usually does." Her hand was tugging at the futile control. She even gave the dashboard a thump with the palm of her hand. She had a dark blue knit hat pulled over her hair. "You can see your breath in this car!"

On cue, a boy behind her made a train whistle noise and started puffing steam and the other children copied. Harriet calmed the coloring box of puffing steam window painters by pointing at the side of the road. Black and white cows stood around in the green. "Look," she said. "Those are the cows we get our milk from."

"Will there be cows when we get there?"

Harriet nodded, "I'm sure there will be, and goats and sheep and ducks also."

Rachel started singing! "Old Mac Donald's Farm," squinting at the window, holding a cow in her fingers held close to her eye. "Old Mac Donald had a farm, ee-i-ee-i. On that farm he had a cow, ee-i-ee-i, with a moo-moo here, a moo-moo there, here a moo, there a moo, ev-erywhere a moo-moo, Old Mac Donald had a farm, ee-i-ee-i-o. Old Mac Donald had a farm—" Car windows gray with rain, drizzle and the window wipers clicking out a steady back and forth beat like a boat rowing through a lake. "And on that farm he had a duck…" Her clarinet voice sang of the pond, paddling with five white ducks and two brown ones standing at the edge, "with a quack-quack here, a quack-quack there—"

Gray winter sky. The black dog was pulling the edge of the blanket on the picnic table, growling, and finally he managed to drag it off, snapping it in its mouth like a flag. A tumble of kids chased it down the hill. Green grass.

"With a bark-bark here, a bark-bark there…" Rachel yipped after the dog, sliding in the wet tall grass and landing on her white sweater. Tug of war with the dog in the waves. A girl with braids pulled on the dog's tail.

Rachel returned up the hill, "Oh no!" She showed her sweatered arm, turned grass green, to her mother.

Behind Glass, out came Harriet with the cake, candles lit, singing, "Happy Birthday to you! Happy Birthday to you!" and the dog left the blanket and the kids came back up the hill, fast as herring to shore.

The hill sloped brown, down into the valley where cows waited like four legged signposts dropped on the field.

Glass ran with a kite, chased by children, bouncing after him.

It took off and soared, pulling string with it like a hooked fish.

"Let me try!" all the children running along with him cried.

He handed the string to a girl with cake chocolate on her fingers. She ran on down the hill, pulling on the clouds. They rushed by him, hopping, running down the hill, watching the bucking kite.

Glass saw Harriet on the hilltop watching Rachel hunting for butterflies. The girl gazelled through the short grass, leaped after an invisible monarch or moth. So he climbed the hill and sat down next to Harriet.

"I'm sorry about what I said at the museum, Glass. I didn't mean to be blunt or cruel."

He knew. But he couldn't say anything at the museum, watching the bird, listening to "Night in Tunisia."

It was okay when her hand took his, "I know how you feel…Your mother was my best friend. I know she has great hopes for you. She wouldn't want you to feel this way."

He answered, "I know, I know."

"When your mother was in the hospital," Harriet was looking down the hill, the shapes of the clouds, "when you were born, she had me take care of your house and what she called The Railroad. Like the Underground Railroad before, only this was during the Vietnam War to help young people your age escape to Canada. She was an amazing person."

But Harriet was too. She had opened his eyes. She showed him what the world could be.

"You know there were raids on the house, they were always suspicious of your house, and always expecting your mother was doing something. But they couldn't catch her in the act. There was always a stranger walking around the block, or a car with men watching the house, and listening in to phone calls. But she persevered for as long as she could."

Harriet was wearing a leafy bracelet that Rachel wove.

"I can't imagine how your mother went through that every day."

Glass almost said out loud, how real his mother still was.

A cry from the hill above, "Look!" and Harriet was on her feet: "Rachel?"

They found the girl kneeling in the weeds, pointing down, "A bird is hurt!"

"A bird?" Harriet sighed. "Let's see, darling." She crouched down next to her, close to the earth. "Oh yesss…"

Glass sat down with her, reached out to the bird. "A sparrow," he said and softly picked it up. He pointed out the wound, "Someone shot him, looks like a BB hole. See?" There was blood on his hand and a feather.

Rachel stared and stroked the air.

Glass could feel its heart beating; it was watching them, but it was fading. "He breathes so fast…shhh." He blew across the wound. "I think he's dying." It was the tree's and wind's loss.

Harriet rubbed her daughter's shoulder and she whispered, "Look up above you. There are so many more birds watching, alive, flying. See?" A tree branch overhead was budded with sparrows. Life's lessons, sad and happy songs. Sounds down the hill of kids kite chasing.

Glass saw the culprits, two boys, the bird

shooters with their guns leaving further down through the grass. "There they go," he said, but they were too far away to scold and too busy searching more trees for more birds to look back at their past victims.

Harriet also saw them, "Yes." She looked at them for a moment, then back to her daughter. She pulled the girl onto her lap. With her head bent over she cradled her girl and whispered things only she could hear.

Harriet in the early morning kitchen light, outside a rolling crayon blue, with a bright star over a streetlamp the last reminder of the night, listening to Glass.

"See, I have this theory that women are the only ones who can save the world." It kept him up through the night thinking, "History keeps repeating with men making the same war over and over."

She nodded, but she put away her smile when she looked into his face and saw that disappointment, and so she said, "Saving the world is something we can all work on together. That begins with equality. Imagine what can grow from that."

She stood up and she smiled. Her hand stopped kindly on his hand, squeezed comfort into his fingers, "Right?"

Where was Lenina? When he was lost out there, she was somewhere else, standing by a window. Silently and not far away, she turned the page and played her music again. It went out drifting on the air.

The myna bird hopped from branch to wire and watched Glass leave for his lunch break. "Chicken on rye!" the bird called to him as he passed. That might have been funny at first, for a bird to give a cannibalistic lunch order, but he was pretty tired of the phrase now and regretted there was no way to un-teach a bird. Every day at noon, it would leap about frantically, urging departers to return with a sandwich.

He scratched the metal cage affectionately as he left and the black feathers responded, leaping from the perch to hold the bars.

Out on the street, the sounds of machines and people: buses, cars, a newspaper tumbling, men hollering down from scaffolding stuck to a brick building, a police woman whistling at a stalled truck in the crowded intersection, and all the tall calico windows carried the sounds.

Glass was walking abstractly, choosing streets randomly, and weaving his way direc-tionless. He liked to test fate this way. Tall walls reached for the clouds, the gray leftovers of yesterday's rain. Maybe he would go into a grocery store and get a juice and some cheese or fruit, pretend he was in Paris, or maybe he would decide to eat lunch in a café. He usually ate lunch with Harriet, but she wasn't at work today. Rachel had a cold.

A herd of people getting off a tour bus stood on the sidewalk, looking lost with cameras, and a kid practicing imaginary archery out the win-dow of an apartment way up overhead. A man selling newspapers was shouting out the headlines, "We Were Provoked!" and "United States Warships Shoot Back!" Santa Claus, uniformed in red and white, rang a bell for money.

By the tall Music Institute building, swirling with cement gargoyles, instruments and stone musical notes, Glass stopped and listened. He heard a violin, floating like a magic carpet down to him.

All the city was stopped and entranced as he looked up the tall ivy tower side to where he saw the open window.

"United States Warships Shoot Back!"

He stepped back. He crossed the street to get a better look inside the window. On the other side of the cars, he stood in front of the Fallout Shelter. It was marked with a black and yellow sign and occupancy number. Now it was used as a Daycare Center. He could hear children playing inside.

Way above, over there, a girl standing next to the window, spinning down notes like Rapunzel hair. He could only see part of her, her sky-blue shirt with her arm seesawing over the bridge, her brown hair and the flashy walnut skin of her violin.

Looking up, with eyes of a moth for the moon, he was suddenly very interested in

Classical music.

"United States Warships Shoot Back!"

The newspaper seller was still calling.

"U.S Jets Down Airliner!"

Glass crossed the street and entered the building past the white marble Mozart and the Beethoven.

Inside, a big poster was pinned on the wall. The Community Orchestra Christmas Concert. He searched all across the small faces of the orchestra photograph, looking for her. There were so many people who weren't her. "No…no…no…" and then he found her.

Proof that time travel was possible; he'd been in the wrong place all his life until now.

Carefully, after surveying the hallway up and down and making sure it was empty, he eased out the stapled edges and the poster was his. "This is crazy!" Rolling it under his arm, he retreated fast through the door, back outside.

The desire to hear her again, see her again, and fall under her spell more completely, made him cross the street quickly. He could listen and look for as long as she was there…She would stop after a phrase of arm weaving creating song and listen to her hidden teacher. Nodding her beautiful four story up head, bringing the violin down to her side where it disappeared beneath the window sill. Glass could see she was talking, though he couldn't hear her voice. He imagined, he was sure, hers was something soft like one of those warm long violin draws of the bow. She nodded, transferring her violin to the other hand to scratch her elbow.

He watched her like a movie camera. Turning the pages, playing, or even yawning, she was the most beautiful person he'd ever seen. It was only beginning, though he told the clouds, leaves and birds, "I'm in love."

Glass had another dream that night about nuclear war. He was standing in a silent city and he looked into the sky. The blue with the white contrail streaks of airplanes flying high. But in a dream's second, glittering missiles appeared.

He yelled at the people around him. People in dreams can be killed too. He yelled at them to run, but they stood there calmly unaware, accepting it or just not caring.

Running through crowded streets, he bumped into her. As if they were victims of a sudden science fiction movie, they hurried down the aluminum stairs of an escalator, going deep into the Earth. He held her hand and pulled her along. "We've got to go underground. We're safe far underground, as far down as this escalator will go!"

And they were going down, further down, opening doors and descending more stairs with the sound of steam machinery getting louder and louder.

A door appeared and opened, surrounding them in sunlight again. They were back on the surface, in time for the sundown.

The sky crunched and became a deep orange.

He held to her as they became atoms and ashes. They met dinosaurs who laughed at them. "We became extinct for you?"

He told them, "We were used. We didn't do this. It's not our fault."

The sounds of a million dinosaurs laughing woke him up out of the nightmare.

Back in this world, he looked at the corner of the room. The Community Orchestra Concert poster was spread like a kite.

He thought of her again and it was alright.

the new world

He knew he must do something about it. Dreams told him time was short. As he walked to the subway entrance, past the poorest people, asking for "spare change" with a few dimes or quarters set on cardboard, all he could think of was finding her.

She left her practice at one o'clock. He found that out last time, watching her longer than he should have, returning late to the museum, giving an excuse that the bus broke down.

Today when lunch time came, he left for break with another excuse for Harriet. Just a smile, as if she knew, she waved him off as he made through the door.

Glass stood across the street in the wintry cool wind. The sky was egg colored white in the blue breath of a farm woman who had picked it from straw to hold up like a moon above her gaze.

When the girl left the window—it was closed because she must have been cold today and so her sound was closed off to him— he watched her disappear and he felt the anticipation nervousness rise and fall in his blood, like the elevator or stairs that must be carrying her back to street level.

He crossed the street to the music building's iron gate entrance and stood outside the castle doorway waiting to be shot into the stratosphere. He heard the steady clicks of her shoes closer on the inside linoleum and he turned his head as casually as a movie cowboy to look, as if he wasn't expecting anything much, maybe just—

But

She was there.

She bloomed alive into his sight, not a little half-body window vision, but an amazing girl. He could only observe her sudden entrance, could only hear her presence, approaching. Trying to be casual, he was shocked at his voice that sounded like a cannon over a blue sea, shot from a battered sinking galleon, "Hello."

She smiled, "Hello," and passed by, bit her soft lip beautifully like a smile trying to hide, and she went by him, carrying her violin case.

Out onto the street, she looked back, or just to swirl her hair carefully behind her ear.

He felt like he'd stood too soon, had been turned into some kind of wobbly shadow after her.

Then he was alive with shooting stars, colors streaking back across and he stepped onto the sidewalk to follow. He felt like shouting for joy. Like origami, her eyes folded him, moved swans in him in ways he couldn't believe. Only she could do that. He wished he could hold her gaze and uncrease it, slow and delicate, to marvel at it, and then fold it back into her again. That was really her walking up ahead, her legs, her walking, and again he wanted to say out loud like a bird singing, "Look at the way she moves!"

He thought of the future when she would be waiting for him to meet her, walking up to her from a distance, seeing her smile grow closer. From afar, her wave would pull him to her like gravity, even stronger than forces of physics, he'd be there at light speed, all the world just a path to her.

She was ahead of him, leaving to the next block, almost to the subway stairs.

He ran after her. The rained on cement. His shoes with no tread left were hard to control. His hands held him from falling by catching the brick wall, as he rushed by green-red glitter window displays, across the street, only watching her, nearly getting hit by a taxi.

She guided him, a lighthouse in his imagination. He was close to rocks, and her guidance went blinking off the street into the subway.

Faster, he ran unsteadily as she disappeared from sight, and not even slowing as he approached the stairway, when he realized, "I'm going too fast!" He tried to grab the handrail to slow himself, smashed into the bar, hands raked across it, he began to fall.

Down the stairs he went tumbling, thumping, bruising on the cement steps.

He reached the landing, where a man curled back further into his handout cardboard corner with wide eyes and cried out, as the great acrobat Glass Benedict Arnold leaped up and windmilled down the few last stairs to the subway platform.

The subway train's doors shut and it started to move slowly caterpillaring along the tracks, as he limped to the turnstile, hit it and got caught up against its pinning bar.

He could see her inside, she was the center of sight now. Sitting at the window, she was watching. Her face was looking at him, like everyone else, except she put her hand to the window. Like a healing hand her palm was up to the glass, as the train slowly moved away.

He was caught up on the turnstile, watching the rumbling, the underground wind turning newspapers over in its hot wake.

Lenina's mother was only sixteen when she was jailed with her father and mother in the desert. A tin and tar roofed hut. The wind came through patched cracks and winter kept the plank walls cold. Her name was Betsy.

He was just out of school and looking for work. He learned carpentry at the camp, but when the walls began to fill, becoming a prison for so many people, he knew what he was a part of. The war was bad enough, this was making it worse.

Standing in that dirt prison with the wind blowing copies of the days' newspapers—Bataan death marches, sinking destroyers, five cent roars for revenge. Seeing people in cages, he started to think.

At the movies, he watched the newsreel relocation of Japanese Americans to the places he built. California's Manzanar and Tule Lake, Arizona's Poston and Gila River, Idaho's Minidoka, Utah's Topaz, Wyoming's Heart Mountain, Colorado's Amache, Arkansas' Jerome and Rohwer: built for hiding, holding 120,000 people. Americans have a history of putting themselves in prisons and reservations. This time, it was General Dewitt who held flame to reason after Pearl Harbor burned and ordered a total evacuation, making enemies out of citizens because, "The very fact that no sabotage has taken place to date is a disturbing and confirming indication that such action will be taken." Knowing what he knew didn't match the music and words of the movie. That truth was too much for him. He wanted to help, he wished now that he could.

It was a miracle to find love there. Whenever he saw her, when they met near the fence every day and he knew he couldn't be apart anymore, they finally flew out of that cage together. They didn't stop until they were deep in the hidden woods of Georgia, far, far, far away from everything, they hoped.

Far, far, far away it seems now, but not so far away in time that memories and pictures couldn't survive. Dreams in family photo albums. Ragged black and white prints and those Polaroids bright as movie colors.

Lenina could remember perfectly the calm of that place in their South, like it was all happening yesterday. She dropped her jump-rope on the grass to run inside the house for supper and running outside afterwards would be returning to the same spot. Raised in the perfect hope that she would fit in beautifully in what was this beautiful world…But her growing up had been sabotaged.

Lenina clearly remembered the day with her father and mother in the car. Lenina in the back seat with the bags, her bare knees tucking up to her chin, her blue dress a rustling noise, and tears. Her father's back to her in the front seat, wearing a red and black plaid jacket, quiet, simply driving the car away down the dusty road, heading for the highways and the airport.

She was angry, sad pouting and tears, looking at his back and hair. He was leaving them.
Not knowing that he was watching in the rear
view mirror, seeing his peaceful world shrink
from sight, disappearing to a dot in the forest
and then gone.

She never saw her father's sorrow before,
until they stopped at The Traveler's Wayside
Temple of the Highway. She looked out the
car window at the small church-like structure
standing next to the pebbled shoulder of the
road. An empty white box shed with a cross
nailed to its sloped roof and a small altar inside.
Her father kneeled inside the small space and
leaned his forehead to his clasped hands against
the altar.

Her breath was fogging the window and she
swiped it clear again with her fingers.

Gray clouds over this highway field of wild
weeds, the prayers were sent skywards.

She rolled down the window wondering if
she could hear him.

Cars rushed by like sighs and then between
the traffic there was a certain silence. Lenina
could hear the whole world. The grass swished
with the cool breeze: the chirp of birds hidden in the weeds and puzzle of tree leaves,

a dog barking, the buzz of a wasp bouncing against the roof, the hush of a high jet, the burbling of her baby sister and her mother's patting hand, the faint whisper of her father. When a car would approach, louder and louder, its roar would rip out everything as it went by, disappearing to let the rest return. The caw of crows, leaves swishing and her father's prayer.

As soon as he got back inside with them, he let his wife drive. Fearing the police, he crouched down low beneath the window under a blanket. That was her father leaving home.

The goodbyes at the airport, watching him watching them watching back, as he went into the airplane and disappeared for the escape north.

The family separated, they grew older apart. Except for letters, or the rare brief weary phone call, he was gone from them.

Until the amazing miracle day twelve years later; he said that enough time had passed there didn't have to be any more running. He was calling them to come to him.

The three of them stopped at his door and dropped their bags.

Lenina knocked, waiting for that father of photos, and she looked back at her mother, tired of such long waiting. In her mother's eyes, her mouth, she knew that the door had quietly opened. They were back as one.

John Coltrane made it through "Love" in eight minutes, but a torrent exists in that space of time. Carried by the feeling of those clacking saxophone keys, Glass dreamed 6:22—6:30.

Glass didn't like danger, not even the thought of it, but there she was: love, perilously close to the edge of it all.

Lenina was standing far above him on the building ledge, with clouds and pigeons beside her. The wind was tugging and pulling her towards falling.

She looked small from where he stood but he saw, he knew it was her, the same way that anyone knows even the smallest of things about the one they love. He knew it was her.

She gripped the concrete outside the window and of course he yelled up to her, "Don't jump! Don't fall!" because she appeared with every shaking second to be losing her hold.

"Don't Fall!" He ran to the building, to the place directly underneath her, cradling her shadow from the hard concrete.

Startled by the flap of pigeons into flight, all at once crumbling off the ledges, fluttering crazily into the air.

"Don't worry, I'm right here!" he shouted up to her.

She slid away from the ledge. Down, she was floating, coming down but drifting as she fell, like a sailboat on the glass blue sky, carried by the strong wind away.

Black smoke from a factory spilled across her. He was running, chasing in her shadow, keeping inside of her blue silhouette on the concrete streets as she sailed above, falling faster. The taste of her mouth in the smoke.

A dream within the dream, a vision where they were together.

Standing on the rocks lining a beach, they watched the green water. It sparkled with a hundred orange backs of fish. They bobbed in the swell of waves that turned inside out and over and over on the beach. The water swept in and out sweetly tossing the goldfish. In the dream within the dream, they watched the fish in the water, until that vision washed away.

Returning to the sight of her separated in the sky, swimming slowly away from him.

It was like chasing the flight of a balloon.

He fell once onto the wet stones, but got up quickly and ran after her shape escaping him, being pulled back by the black clouds that swirled her away. Buildings blocked him in. He ran up against a wall.

She was leaving over the bricks, disappearing, angeling down out of sight. A trail of smoke followed her like a burning plane. It charcoaled after her and that faded away too.

Glass clawed at the wall that wouldn't budge. What he was most afraid of was happening.

The only way to stop it was waking up.

careful

"How can I possibly face her again after that?" Glass worried.

Falling like some slapstick clown, watching helplessly as the subway pulled away from him, burrowing into the tunnel till it was gone in blackness, and how he had to pull himself up the railing back into the light of day.

He would have to admit solemn as a Confederate gentleman handing over his sword that he had been defeated. Craziness, walking back to work along the pavement and imagining there underneath his footsteps, she must be wandering further pulled along in her train. The clacking, whirring electric-blue rolling of wheels underground.

His knee hurt when it bent with every step.

"President Sends Troops" blared the day's headlines at a newsstand, and glossy covers showed dark armed gunboats, soldiers carrying guns and airplanes with missiles. Glass stopped and read the print, "In an effort to ease the tensions and bring peace to this unstable area, the president today announced plans to send a limited number of marines as a peace-keeping force. 'It is in our best interests as a non-aggressive democratic nation to send these troops as a symbol of our resolve to achieve peace,' the president in a letter to the press stated earlier today." The report went on, but Glass backed away from the sick words in horror and limped towards the museum.

He wanted away from all this doomed falling. Falling after a girl in the cellophane light of a falling city…A skywriting plane had written something in huge upside down white smoke letters that faded slowly above.

People can still remember March 23, 1942. When they were the only ones given the curfew and their town was entirely shut off to them like an 8:00 PM to 6:00 AM cage. They were prohibited from leaving their homes while police and committee groups drove past to make sure. Watching from their windows, the streets were otherwise bare except for the stray, quietly strange, foreboding.

Every night Betsy kneeled with the gray blanket wrapped tightly round her shoulders looking out the dark glass. People who lived on the water were ordered to put black paper on their windows so they couldn't signal Japan. So she barely breathed, afraid that police would see her, looking through the folds of curtain.

Moonwhite in her shining hair. The black car that approached every night at this time was feeling its way past, the wheels turning slowly up the street. The headlights glazed across the neighborhood windows, leaping shadows. The shingles on roofs glittered diamonds. When she saw the driver was watching her, the dark shadow of his hat, she froze and held her breath. The look took long seconds as the car crept, panthering down the street. When she curled fitfully, finally into sleep, she dreamed that she was something in the zoo.

Step by step, the U.S went to war with itself. The next law was the five mile net that closed in. Without permission from the authorities, no one was allowed outside that five miles into the other America. Roadblocks, police, soldiers and fences would make sure.

Betsy would spend hours at the beach listening to the soothing rush of waves on the sand. Her tears there with the thoughts of life becoming a prison—"I don't understand! I don't understand!"—the salt of sea on her skin, the damp stickiness of sand. How could she ever be the enemy? Her hair dried slowly, black shining over her shoulders. The sea was so big, how could Japan ever reach over?...Once she wished for a great fleet of Japanese ships to plow over the horizon, their pearly hulls shining in rising sun, with their engines beating like great hearts. Across the sea from Japan, an endless fleet of ships that would anchor close to shore with their guns pointed at America and then a heroic voice would call from the biggest ship, "You have mistreated the people who left our shores. You have betrayed these peaceful, hard-working people." She dug shapes with her heels into the soft beach, letters spelling out *S.O.S.*

Newsreels and newspapers. Rules and laws were passed. War made a country crazy. Stamping people as good or bad. When that happens, the end has begun.

Remember April 1942. They were ordered to evacuate their houses within five days, to proceed to their designated Assembly Center, taking only what could be carried.

No one could believe what was happening, and what terrible thing would be next. Leaving their houses, their lives, emptying their rooms onto the street curb. The cars and trucks that descended into their neighborhoods—she remembered that man who didn't have to worry about curfews and camps, looking over their things. When her father sold their refrigerator for three dollars, offering his hand to shake on the agreement, that man ignored the gesture. The hate in his eyes, turning his attention to the bargain and with the help of his two sons, pushed it up into the back of their truck.

Able to have only what could be carried—she heard that someone down the street sold their car for ten dollars. She held a suitcase, a movie-stars magazine filled with "Buy War Bonds!" ads, a glass tube of beach sand (not knowing that where she was going there was plenty of sand). She wore a necklace made from a handful of seashells, slowly fading sea-colored purples, blues and greens.

The Temporary Assembly Centers were racetracks and fairgrounds. People were herded into animal stables. Betsy remembered her best black shoes standing on the wood chips. They were surrounded by an eight foot tall grid of barbed wire fence, with watchtower corners and uniformed guards. Searchlights and .30 caliber machine guns. No applause in these places anymore. Bleachers worn by stamping feet were turned on end to become walls. Condemned to those same stalls where only months before blue ribbon cows and hogs were displayed.

When they arrived, her father's strong grip on her hand was torn away as they were separated into two lines. Men and women, left and right. She was crying as her mother stroked her dark hair, "Don't worry." She had to open her mouth for a nurse who poked around her tongue. She had to take off her shirt for her spine exam. Rough pinching along her arms while someone looked into her eyes with a bright light. She cried during the examination, while her mother whispered over to her, "Don't worry."

At night, candles splashed on the plank walls of the stall, the heavy blanket pulled across the doorway opening creased with dark moving shadows. The smell of animals and the night sounds of everyone trying to sleep. Her mother's coughing began. She watched from under her rough blanket, pulled up over her nose. Her father kneeled beside the candle light, carefully writing a letter to the president, his slow hand writing. *The safety of America is threatened by mothers and children, their husbands and fathers?* It was better to be blind than to use sight to create an enemy. The War Relocation Authority created their enemy and kept them caught in ten traps across the country, from East to West. Trains and buses with their windows painted black, trucks covered over in tarps, brought all these people from the fairgrounds to the concentration camps.

When Betsy remembered these times, it was another place she saw and she was another person. No one could believe stepping out of the bus at the camp that they were going to become part of this sand. A Boy Scout troop held flags and a welcoming band played "God Bless America." Barbed wire walls and tar paper roofs, the camp looked like a place to be forgotten forever.

Dust after dust, white in the wind. Her mother took her into their shack; they were hushed by the gray bareness of it. Her father would stand near the fence under the shadow weight of a watchtower, looking away at the far rise of brown mountains. With the tube of sea sand in her hand she resolved that somehow she would leave, they would never keep her here. Somehow she knew there would be a way for her to escape.

The chance would come when she had nothing left. After her mother died of TB, after her father died two weeks later, she was all alone.

In the dust, the tires left tracks between the sharpened fences. The students passed by in front of his truck and he radioed her. Their eyes had been looking at each other for weeks, waiting for the rest of them to meet.

She stopped, close for a moment at his opened window, pretending to look through her notebook and she whispered into the paper, "Tonight." She walked on back away, the swirl of sand from the stopped wheels drifted by.

It caught him by surprise—for the first time he was making a new life for two. He dropped off supplies to the kitchen and left back out of the camp's gates with the plan of night occupying his mind.

From the moment he saw her, he knew they were connected. They hardly knew each other beyond a feeling and a few weeks of passed notes, but he believed they were meant to be together. Not in this desert though. Escape out of this world, into the making of their own.

Pale as a paper, the moon had been left in the blue meadow sky.

Glass ran to his second grade class to watch rockets take off from Florida and land on the moon. The open door let lemonade sunlight fall inside. The big room was dark but a TV was on. The teacher invited him in. "History in the making!" she said. A rocket was leaving for the moon while the teacher was eating her lunch. He watched for a while and left back outside, down the wooden steps, along the tar looking into the blue far above, looking for the rocket's tail...

He went back to the fence, his fingers clung

to the mesh wire chain link fence, watching through to the other side, down the tarred slope to that big broad pavement plateau where there were firetrucks shooting water at people. Hard streams of water and police with riot gear, barking dogs, plastic shields and visors. Screams and broken glass and flying rocks; tear gas drifting like a fog. And there were the children watching with him, from up above, with only a fence between them and down below.

This is what they wanted him to learn, so he was learning young at school with the rest of the confused first graders, the ways of the 1972 world.

Another war with Asia, bullet-sized rain rang on the street, and Glass' mother ran. Her feet splashed through the dark. The light of the neighborhood houses shined warm from behind drawn curtains. Her jeans were muddy and green from the fall on the lawn.

She knew he would get away. It was her they were after. They had been watching her and waiting for the right time. Dogs barked. She had a feeling that the time had come. She knew this was it. She was so tired.

A car accelerated quickly; waves tossed out from the wheels. White yellow headlights blinded her. She stopped, captured in the haunting blaze and she didn't even scream as it knocked her over and tore away from the crumple shining in its wake. It was an imagining that Glass Benedict Arnold had long felt; he saw a dark night, with the rain falling like a firing squad.

When Harriet told him that wasn't how it happened it shattered him.

"There are truths people never want to know. I understand it hurts, but it helps to see. She told me she was running out of time. I'm haunted I couldn't help her more. I'm sorry I let you believe something else. It was night, that's true, and it was raining."

Rain and wind. A dead branch beat against the garage. A gunshot jumped from the house.

Every time they stopped, Betsy had to slide down into the cramp in front of her car seat and hide under a wave of blanket like the memory of the ocean back home. Into gray water, looking across a long green splash west to Japan…There was a land that felt like such a dream—knowing it only through the magic bedtime stories her mother told at night—folktales from Japan about birds and turtles, dragons and cranes, talking rice pots, bamboo and yams, foolish and wise people. The cool breeze blew her black hair, her hand shading her eyes, thinking about that faraway land. "Go home!" "Why don't you go back!" the yells and looks whenever she went into town. She couldn't understand how that Japan could be her home, "Do they speak English in Japan?"

Feet on wet sand, she walked to the sea, letting her blue dress pull up over her shoulders, slip over her head and the cloth floated out of her hand. Thin, only fifteen years old, she left her dress on the beach as she stepped like a heron into the surf. The curl of cold foam ran across her feet. Up, up the water climbed as she walked in deeper, over her legs, waist. The cold water ate over her and she waited. Shivering…she looked down into the wavy pale, at her underwater legs and she joined her reflection. She sunk herself in. She swam in the cold, eyes open to the sting of the salt. She kicked and pushed at the press of underwater. There was so much power in the ocean, it could carry her somewhere far-away, somewhere else. The sea didn't want her though. She floated and listened to the buzzing undersea motor, wishing there was a fishing boat to take her aboard and take her to a dream Japan. It wasn't happening. She let the water drive her back to shore.

the book of elbows and knees

The Christmas Community Concert hall was crowded as a garden and he watched through every person there, looking for her. The stage was set with empty folding chairs. Which one would be hers? Which side of stage would she enter on? A motion behind the curtain. Was that shape her? Was she a velvet wave?

All the talk in the hall hushed as the musicians appeared. Black dresses and black suits. Where was she? She may not have come, he worried. She could be ill, she could have stayed home. No sign of her. He wondered if she— then *"There she is..."* he whispered, as she walked in.

A bright ray of light slid across and she gave a nervous smile as she glanced at the audience, holding the violin to her side.

She brushed at her lap as she sat and placed the violin across her legs. She looked at the crowd, the light in her eyes. A smile seemed to fly for him. Who knows if she was looking for him too? She smiled at the nutty conductor who entered and everyone was clapping now.

Glass was still clapping for her.

Once he was sitting, he couldn't see her around the other player who raised her violin up on cue. So far, he could only see her knees and arm. He wanted to make a book of all her beauty and wonder and call it *The Book Of Elbows And Knees.*

When the music began, he watched it swim in her.

Glass couldn't stop watching everything about her. Her arm would twist just slightly. She was the one making the sound so beautiful. He wondered about this music that must have been two hundred years old and still someone like her could come along and bring it to life. He couldn't doubt that she could be anything less than everything.

Glass even saw his mother turn in the seat in front of him to smile back at him. But he didn't want to miss the girl with the violin. When the orchestra stopped and everyone applauded, he watched her rest. She tugged at the shoe strap at the back of her heel. Such was the wonder of her, all the little things were new and marvelous. Watching her was magic.

His mother turned round in her seat to look at him again, her arm over the curve of chair back. This time he heard her tell him, "Sometimes this is all you need. You show the universe when you're in love." And before the conductor started them rolling again, she said, "I like her too."

Christmas bells shook in back of the orchestra. It sounded like a sled driving in the snow.

Soon he would say her name, "Lenina."

Under a cover of darkness, the city turned wax; green, white, yellow lights seeped out of black office blocks. On the way to the museum, Glass stopped at the TV repair shop window. Televisions glowed like cabbages in the closed store. They all showed the same old movie, but he pictured her across the row instead. He saw her smiling face multiplied.

In ten minutes he was somewhere else and the sky was bright yellow, lemon, no clouds just a whirlpool of warm light above. He closed his eyes.

Moving along, when he opened his eyes, a green land went endlessly in front of him.

Clouds, blue sky, even birds—so many of them stayed in that blue sky. Another few steps and he was walking in forest. The museum walls were covered with windows to other places. The next display was a meadow. A deer watched him. A minute passed and he was painted in that peaceful place too. On a long night, he could be in a hundred beautiful worlds.

The sudden flutter of wings out of dark landed next to his ear.

The Passenger Pigeon sat on his shoulder. It rested long enough to look into his eyes. He had time to think, "All this time that bird's been alive!" Then it left him, across the room, out an open window.

The museum melted away as he ran outside, down the steps along the path, looking up into the sky between buildings. Glass had one last chance to see the bird when he reached the corner. The pigeon was sitting on a lamppost, preening its blue feathers. It took off when he called. It swooped away and vanished into the shadows of the park.

The last Passenger Pigeon was gone.

Glass stared at the dark shapes of the trees. The park was like another painted museum display. Artists recreated the dream feeling of a

winter city park at night. Another lonely looking place…until someone else was there with
him.

A girl with a violin.

They were both yawning at the same time,
the lateness of the night catching up with them
both. Seeing her was like remembering to
breathe.

She stood there in a long coat looking at
him, a slight swing of her instrument case, and
an umbrella in her other hand. "Hello," she
smiled.

"Hello…"
She said, "Hello again."
Had it started to rain? Did that just happen?
The water twinkled on the fabric of her coat.
The street lamp made them sparkle like diamonds. The barrette in her hair shined and he
thought of all the times he had seen them glitter on the sidewalks, lost off girls. She laughed
and opened her umbrella. He never met a girl

with an umbrella.

There was a corner store ahead. Fruits, vegetables, flowers lined up along the storefront, bright colors under the yellow and green night lights.

It was really starting to pour now.

How long had they just been standing there?

The rain and wind washed the colors down into rainbow lit puddles and streams, wrinkles of reflections spread to dancing with the wind. The raindrops sounded like telephones ringing on the tin roofs of cars parked along the curb.

A yellow taxi moved by them, slow as a swan.

She was caught off guard when her umbrella filled with wind. For a moment it seemed she would blow away down the street. Pulled by the gust, she held the wind in her hands. Like a cartoon, she might have flown off her feet until he helped.

The umbrella came down between them and they were back.

Water lilies shipwrecked on a pond. Waiting for her while the rain rusted the city.

Another second and she looked away. She did, he did, and then they looked at each other again and laughed.

"Come on!" she told him.

Rain splattered his face, ran into his mouth and eyes, as he ran with her. What song had just started? Something he never heard before.

When they stepped under a canopy, a stream waterfalled from the torn curtain. The rain turned the city into a whole other world. A hundred sounds of water, whistling, tapping, dancing, drumming, dripping, plopping, clicking, trotting, sloshing, and purring.

Talking with her had its own motor, every sentence had direction and silence had meaning too.

As the rain stopped, the world around them calmed. The wet wheels of cars, people running with newspapers over their heads. As soon as he noticed all the flowers surrounding them and realized they were in a flower shop, he turned and said, "I'd like a bouquet of flowers, please."

The woman with the smock collected the flowers together, wrapped them with paper and string. She smiled. She was used to this sort of thing. She passed him the flowers and he paid. The ring of the register floated like a cathedral bell.

Over the streets Christmas ornaments and colorful lights were strung. Wreathes dripped green water.

"I got you some flowers," he said.

"Oh, thank you!" She tried to hold the juggle of flowers, the umbrella and her violin, and as he tried to help her hold it all, their fingers met. "Thank you, thank you," she showed him the softest look. Then, "Can you believe the weather? All of a sudden we need an ark! Oh—" she stared again, "these flowers are beautiful, so marvelously wonderful. My giraffe will love them!" she laughed. He didn't doubt that she might have one.

"Well," she said, "let's go find someplace inside. We can go to a café or something?"

"Yes, that would be perfect," he agreed. He was with her—all this was so simple. They walked, hopped puddles together. She landed on her heel and he caught her arm.

Bumping shoulders. When he talked with her, he was swimming or flying a kite.

He said, "It's funny, just yesterday the world felt like I was lost in the loneliest movie."

"Me too."

"You too?"

"Mmhmmm," she nodded.

"Oh, I'm sorry. Well, it's a good thing we met each other."

"Yes!"

"Here," he said. "Let's pretend this door is taking us somewhere we've never been before."

"It is!" she smiled.

They stepped into the entrance of a restaurant. Another bell rang. They laughed at all the water they brought inside.

She put her umbrella and violin down on the seat of their booth, sat down with the flowers beside her. She said, "When you fell at the subway—"

"Don't worry about that. I've been falling for a long a time. I just wanted to talk to you..."

She reached her hand across the table to him. "Well, now you can."

He held her damp hand. He rubbed her hand between his and he turned the soft palm over. He could see her story in her hands. He traced a finger along a crease of her palm. West of her thumb, then he moved it east, thinking of all the life he held.

Her fingers closed up around his finger and she held his hand. She gave him a squeeze. "Your hand is nice," she said.

The window shined with the falling rain. Now the storm was like watching a movie. They ordered some food while the water pawed against the plate of glass. It was like he was on another planet and he thought it was so funny he put down his fork and laughed.

"What are you thinking?" she asked him.

He reached across the table for her violin hand.

"I've been alone forever. If I was an astronaut, this whole world happened just because of you." She told him she was a seer, she could predict his arrival like radar. Not always though—earlier in the day, he tapped her shoulder when she didn't see him, "Oh hello!" her eyes sparked when she turned. He gave her a book with a message inside: For you. This is a gift for all the birthdays of your life I missed—all your growing up years, painting stones and Mayan tapestries, while I was floating miles away, digging for dinosaur bones and climbing green trees.

She gave him a Fortune Fish. She put it on his palm and it curled. The red paper fish shape that rolled on his hand told a story. "You're in love," she told him, reading the directions. Yes, well, what could he say?

"I remember this family down the street from me. I must have been 6 or 8 years old and this boy was showing us around his house. He wanted us to see the disaster of his house. I remember the living room was just littered with things. There was a model car kit that his older brother had been working on, some plastic yellow dragster car with bright decals. The ripped cardboard box it had come in. Things were just strewn all over, pillows ripped apart, broken furniture and glass, bottles and cans on the carpet. The window curtains were all drawn shut so it was sort of dark, but you could tell this was a family disaster. And another image, probably the main image that I still carry with me, was sitting there on that glass coffee table. There was a big jug wine bottle with a candle shoved into the mouth of it. And this candle had dripped all its bright wax down the side of the glass like bleeding rainbows. I remember being so scared of that room. It was destroyed like a war. I couldn't understand what happened. That boy's parents were gone, he was left on his own, and we went outside, chalk pictures on the cement, sounds of kids playing. We followed a path through the trampled grass to the back alley where it was so narrow we had to walk sideways, pressed close to the wet concrete shadows and spider webs and in there he showed us this dead waterlogged rat. I used to have to carry these things in me, as rusting metal nightmares. I used to feel I had to be afraid of so much and especially love. But all that…" he began to smile. "That was before I knew that it's only love that keeps things working at all here on Earth. Before I knew you, I was only waiting to find that out."

She said, "I thought about the things you said after I hung up the phone and I couldn't sleep. I was so happy."

He knew the feeling. Waiting for the new day to start, watching the clock at 2:56 AM, waiting for the light so he could see her again. The night was long as an ocean. Late, the wind rattling the window and rain hitting the pane like jazz notes. The time without her was gray as the Atlantic. How could he sleep without thinking of her? He closed his eyes and she chased him through dreams. He asked her if she thought it was possible to meet each other in dreams. She told him, "I already have. I had a dream you were climbing a tree." He imagined himself in her dreams, what a world that would be. And he thought of all the times she had been in his dreams already and wondered if they crossed paths.

He reached out in the air and touched where Lenina's forehead would be. All he could say was, "Take care," but meaning of course the old Sea Shanty, "be ever so careful and let no harm ever happen to you, stay happy and healthy and hurry back over the blue," when what he really wanted to say was, "I love you."

He loved to visit her room. She made a world in there. There was museum light on everything he wanted to know about. He was drawn in easily, pulled by the force the way a bee falls into a flower. He could feel the magic of time—things she saved from childhood were there, drawings, paintings, photos, schoolwork, music programs beginning in 5th grade until now. He wished he had always been with her, and he didn't want to miss anything more. There just wasn't enough time—it went by like a dream—it was a dream. He sat close to her and showed her an old picture and she laughed.

He knew what made her laugh and preserved it like a firefly in a jar, waiting to reopen it for her just to watch her reaction. "Hey!" he touched her foot. The brown sock thread was worn and her toes showed through. He was in love with her to the ends of her body. "Yes, I know," she said. The gleam of her teeth when she laughed. "I've had these since the ninth grade." Listening to her records.

Today between subways he heard someone and thought it was her laugh.

To be close enough to smell her, or stroke her sweater arm, touch her leg in conversation. And she would do it too! She even showed him card tricks, where he was surprised to pick the Ace of Hearts and then he rediscovered it hidden up her sleeve. He was more and more in love with her, watching everything about her, looking deep into her eyes when she spoke. He felt dopey as Henry Fonda in one of his romantic 1940s Paramount pictures. That happy feeling being with her; it could lift him, walk him through walls and reveal secrets.

In her room, looking at the clock and seeing it was 2:04 AM and she said, "I thought it was around 12!" and they had been talking for five hours through the night into the morning. "See you tomorrow!" she laughed.

Yellow tulips grew beside someone's front steps. Nobody seemed to notice as he pretended to tie his shoe next to the cluster and after a car passed, he quickly reached over and snapped a tulip free. He held the green stem close under his jacket, the yellow petals were safe cupped in his hand. He went to her door, knocked— no answer—so he peeked inside and saw her sleeping, sock feet sticking from the covers, and he quietly closed the door. Pulling tape off the bulletin board in the hall, he taped the tulip to her door. When he came back an hour later to check, the flower was gone and she sat inside in a red plaid bathrobe. Still sleepy, the flower bent with the weight of her "Good morning!" on the table next to her. "It's wonderful!" The way she said that, the words were around her like a necklace. If he didn't think about her, he'd go crazy.

"We walk to a movie theater at night. Of course we're holding hands. The name, Dream Theatre is spelled in neon light. *Charade* is playing. Cary Grant and Audrey Hepburn. We go inside. They have red carpeting. I ask if you want popcorn."

"And I say yes," she said.

"Okay. Oh, they also have a table in the lobby with a big silver urn full of orange spice tea. So we take our paper cups and popcorn and we go up a ramp to the balcony."

"What are the seats like?"

"Oh! Those great old overstuffed ones that bounce a little back and forth. The theater was built in 1920. Charlie Chaplin used to be there. We're pretty excited, talking and waiting for the big curtains to open. When they do, all of sudden, the movie begins."

"What happens in it?"

"Oh, well…" She had him there. It had been a while since he saw that film.

"*Oh, well,*" she repeated, teasing him and

laughed.

"Um, I remember the fairground scene with the music and people spinning around and she is running frantically. I remember some of the story. He's chasing her through the subway. She's hiding on the train and he leaps on just in time. He's wearing a white coat and she's in a yellow coat. She sees that he notices her. When the train stops, they're off again, running through the tunnels. She hides in a phone booth and he's searching…and off they go again. Guns are drawn, two men behind pillars. 'Trust me!' He promises. Then the drums again, more running, the clatter of her shoes and more music until they arrive…In a theater, deserted, dark…She's almost discovered… Then Cary Grant pulls A-4, the correct latch for the trapdoor and down falls the killer… One of those Hollywood endings."

Lenina had pictures all over her and all around her, spilled out photo albums from both their families. All told stories with visions. They were putting together all these pieces. Like a puzzle laid out before them, she watched and felt it take shape slowly. Glass said, "She had a plan." Their reality was beautiful; together they were making it magical.

She watched her lover through her sleepy eyes and she felt him touch her with the scraps of paper.

On the flow of her bare skin and along her outline on the blanket next to her, he hovered over, placing little colored squares, old black and white or sepia. He would show her a photo of a sailor and his wife from long ago and say, "They were leading to you…" putting it by the dark wave of her hair. Sometimes he asked her questions about her relatives, "Who's this?" Someone holding flowers. She would smile, tell him sleepily who and kiss, then he would find a place for that photo. And so he built their family tree on into the night. Through her window drapes rocked the sycamore, the stars, dark and moon, all wondering what would happen next.

America in fifty years or so will be very different. Glass and Lenina's granddaughter was flying back from Japan. All that water was only a puddle. She looked over the silver wing and saw land. When the wheels sat down on the new world concrete, she held her breath. The airport glowed out the oval window. Everyone headed for the open silver door. She left the plane struggling to carry a heavy bag filled with books of poetry.

When Lenina and Glass Benedict Arnold walk in the park together, it's Christmas and he has slipped a hand inside one of her mittens, sharing her warm hold. She wraps his fingers tight inside the wool.

Lenina says, "Today almost smells like summer." She is shining like a movie.

"You're right, it does."

There it is in the air. A taste of salt, sound of waves, green shadows, porch swings, with a lazy hammock in the leaves. More than a million flowers are humming under the soil, waiting to bloom.

He is staring at the breeze in her brown hair, with red and black in it too. He imagines how far that little breeze came to be with her. He was imagining a lot. Anytime she got close he was in something like water being swept away by the tide. Silky waves would take him out to sea and she was a long time lingering.

The park is quiet, just their feet crunching dry leaves, the sounds of their talking, laughing, and the sounds of them alone on the path. There are birds and contrails in the sky. Being with her, there aren't any fears for the world. Everything in her—the fire in her eyes, flash of a smile, burn of her closeness, and the spark when she touches his hand—is all that matters.

She wants to stop by the water and drops his hand to run over to the fountain. Frozen leaves caught under a thin crackle of ice.

He put a hand on her. He can feel her thin shoulder beneath the warm thick layers of sweater and wool. She wraps her plaid scarf around him too and they sit lassoed together on the ledge, looking into the pool.

She traces her mitten round the outline skeleton of a frozen leaf. "I'm thinking of the tree this leaf came from."

Glass turns. "One of the trees around here." Most of the leaves have fallen. The trunks and branches could have been painted with a black brush. "When we come back in the spring, we can see all the leaves again."

"And how will that be?" she asks.

"Animals, trees, birds, everything. The most peaceful place in the world."

IN THE SUBWAY CITY

*The New York City Journal
of
a 23 Year Old Scientist*

———

INTRODUCTION

This comes as a complete surprise to me! I had no idea I kept a journal in NYC, until I uncovered this on a recent basement excavation. In early 1989, New York City welcomed me with Statue of Liberty arms. The cold cartoon world there was pretty inspiring and all those ghosts gave me new confidence in writing. It's interesting archaeology to see how some of these passages reappear in the fiction first half of this book. The journal ends in the Arctic, a little before I left the city that summer.

A DAY IN THE LIFE OF THE GREAT ZORBINA

Planes are dropping out of the sky

Please apologize for me and offer her a dozen roses. AT LEAST SING HER THE LATEST STEVIE WONDER SONG! She sounded very removed from the traffic jam of reality when I told her my name was "Fritz…Fritz." I hope I didn't cause her any undue confusion or remorse. Again my deepest apologies and if I was Tony Orlando I'd simply say, "Darling, if I had a yellow ribbon…and you were an oak tree." In other words, give her the Purple Heart of Understanding, the Declaration of Wonderocity, etc. etc. etc.

A Day in the Life of the Great Zorbina is difficult now that they took her silver trailer away. True, it was falling apart at the seams, crushed as a lightbulb from the Titanic, disappeared under the brown and green ivy. Still, she knew where the door was. That was her home.

She could jumpstart a mule with that look

Feb 2, 1989

Let me say something else about The Great
Zorbina. She wore an eyepatch. Not because
she was blind. She could see too much with
that eye. Everything. You could have ice skated
on her insight.

Her voice when she laughed, "You weirdo!"
over the telephone.

An evening of hieroglyphics; an accordion
would have had trouble figuring it out.

Why did they take The Great Zorbina's trailer
away? She didn't have to worry about paying
the rent, that's for sure.

With more to gain than a dinosaur's tie size.

Feb 3, 1989

A wallflower meets a shadow

Feb 4, 1989

¾ of an airplane conversation:
"I've got *Cosmo, People, Us*
and Bertolt Brecht."

An x-ray of a sandwich

Feb 5 & 6, 1989

A Bermuda Triangle
where Amelia Earhart sleeps

Feb 7, 1989

She could have been 12 feet tall
standing at the end of a swimming pool

Feb 8, 1989

Columbus on the subway

Fishing in a wishing well
The Great Zorbina found
Spanish galleon remains

A babushka
worn on a rocking chair

What does an old Russian
with two gold teeth
buy at the grocery store?

   1 pack of 80 cheese ravioli
   2 Little Debbie chocolate Devil Squares
   1 strawberry ice cream
   1 Swanson's Fish 'n Chips
   1 sour cream

While a blue Lenin watches
from the freezer window

The wind helped itself
to an ice cream cone

Strange to think you knew me
but I didn't know you
or your beautiful black hair
and I still don't know you!

She burned down my Drive-In

Feb 10, 1989

It could have been September
the way she said hello

She walks like a ship flying at half mast

The way he follows you around
and wants to be your shadow
like a forged Rembrandt painting

If your comfort came packaged
it would cost more than $1.98

Finding out why Houdini
locked himself in a box

Looking for an apartment:
*All the creature comforts of
an iguana glued to the black keys
of an accordion.*

So tired…into a curious sleep
like the ghosts of the Confederacy
examining a unicycle

Little Red Riding Hood takes the A Train

No one's here
a playground cemetery

Everything on top of the ground
came from below (all the cement,
glass, marble, metal and plastic)
even that McDonalds

She sleeps with a cup of
White Rock Purity Ginger Ale.
The snow and trees outside.
She is wrapped up
like an orange.

She's reading *In Defense of
The October Revolution.*
I try to stop watching her.

The desire for a plastic pear

Rush hour trains
slow metal dreams

Bela Lugosi is serving
sandwiches and drinks
to unknowing travelers
in his Transylvania diner car

Too many chimneys
have gone into making
this town
I would have preferred
elephants

Feb 11, 1989

It's hard to move
with a grand piano
in my head

Feb 12, 1989

Chinese New Year
Rivers and firecracker boats

Feb 13, 1989

He said, "Even thieves respect the church."
Cut to bleeding face of Jesus in the window.

Feb 14, 1989

She was wearing glasses

Someone through the wall is playing
a doomed piano, the faucet is sinking,
the baby upstairs just stopped crying.

All the people walking in a city

The Great Zorbina was in the city
and she felt sorry for the dogs.

A rabbi with a cowboy hat

At 1:28, the rocking chair remembers
the forest and becomes a tree again

These footprints of the 20th Century

The hero crosses the lawn
to the sound of a factory whistle

The Great Zorbina cried when she saw
the display at the American Museum of
Natural History. Everything was frozen
behind glass like a postcard where
the words are spelled in green moss,
with birds and deer and trees:
The Olympic National Forest

I've seen those eyes in old movies

The ghost of Fred Astaire
tried to teach the pipes
in this apartment to tango
but they kept skipping their lessons
going to the horse track instead.
Now the radiator taps like hooves.

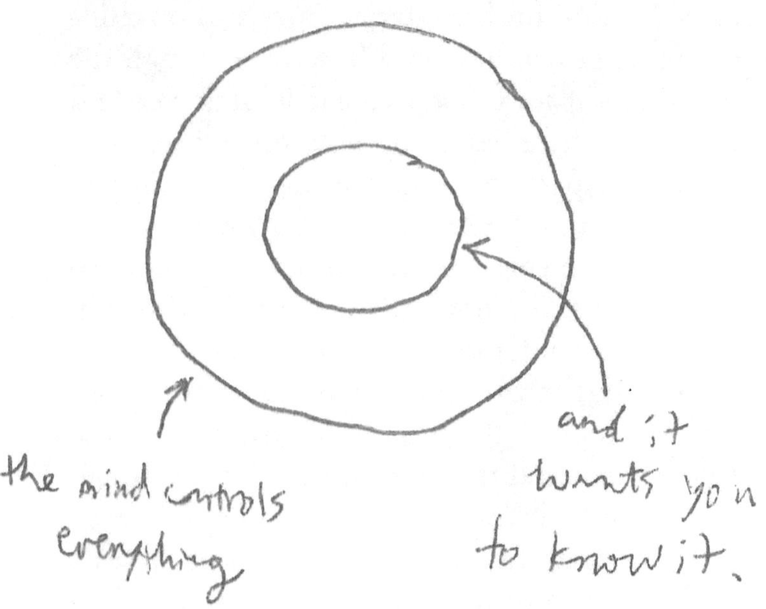

Feb 17, 1989

Japanese butterfly wings

Coney Island's tall metal flower rusting up over the sand overlooks a fenced off lot, where its shadow sounds like pollen on the chain link. There's an opening in the fence, pulled aside wire like a circus tent flap. On the ground are cans, bottles, broken glass, stones and machinery parts grown like wild flowers. Through the opening, the lot is big, as if a field of flowers did once sleep here before moving on. An octopus ride, unhappy looking, waiting for summer, curled to rest beside a wooden falling down wall. All the space of the ground is littered so walking is really navigating and it is winter in Coney Island. Close by is a stack of mattresses, carpets and tarps, tented like canvas pancakes. An opening like the mouth of a sad clown close to the earth and it is dark inside. Coney Island hiding under carpets. On my hands and knees I peek inside and for only a second a dog appears in the light. A brown dog with white striped on its face appears crouching like a magical animal and then it is gone, disappeared back into the black of Coney Island under carpets.

Feb 18, 1989

The rose told him, "Pain doesn't bother me," and claimed her great grandfather invented barbed wire. While he wondered what that meant, it was too late, he was already caught on her thorns.

A movie cowboy lights matches off anything. Off his shoe, off someone's horse, off the back of a waiter. He can get fire out of anything. He keeps a match under the rim of his white hat, always ready to show off.

Feb 19, 1989

A secretary who works beside the subway line
doesn't even look up from her typewriter
as the train goes by

A tree on 11th Street begged The Great Zorbina for some leaves, or flowers, or whatever she could spare

A caste system of jobs

Little America

Feb 20, 1989

The music of the spheres is a million angels knitting scarves and sweaters. You stop like a telephone pole and hum. You need no other nourishment than that astronomy sound.

Walking along the sidewalk past a building emptying itself out, dust, saws and radio salsa, there are two animal heads on the sidewalk in front of her. One is a boar's head and the other is a small deer. Both taxidermy heads are mounted on wooden plaques and stare up at the blue sky. The Great Zorbina peeked inside the doorway and a workman covered in dust looked at her for a moment. He passed her a huge deer head. She accepted the bouquet of fur and bones and kept walking. Except now that she was walking with a dead deer's head in her arms, she needed to know what she was going to do with it. Like a sacred Egyptian secret involving pyramids and tombs, she hadn't the faintest idea. She kept walking as if this was no antler mystery, she was only carrying a bag of groceries. Nobody seemed to notice it was anything else. One ear was unpeeling and the fur was matted overall with dust. The eyes were cloudy as stones. They were not the royal jewels that once saw forest and lakes. It was better that the eyes couldn't see where she was going, down into the L Street Station. She set the deer's head by her feet and paid a dollar for a token. Then she carried her guest through the turnstile and onto the platform to wait for the uptown train. Where would a deer be at home? There was no dark picnic of forest, and after all these years it was used to walls, but she thought of the dark silence that grew like tree shadows in these tunnels. The Great Zorbina found it a spot up on a ledge where it could observe without being seen.

Red splatters on the floor and two streaks of blood on the orange seat. I make a quick exit off the train at the next subway stop.

The New York Public Library at 42nd Street isn't even a library! It's a dictionary of noise. I wanted to ask, where are the books? But I know if I did I'd be flogged from A to Z.

She talked like she was on stilts.

The Great Zorbina was walking, looking for the West 4th Street subway, somewhere past all the purple flags of NYU, watching the people river by. A dwarf walked along the edge of the street on the edge of the crowd, wearing a black studded leather jacket, and gone with the tide the next moment.

I forgot about my 9 o'clock interview until 11 o'clock.

"I'm what you call homeless." Wearing army green and the 3 o'clock subway glaze.

In between sitting there reading *People* magazine, she answers the phone like a pleasant hamburger, or she passes out clipboards to applicants. I told her I was interested in office work and she gave me a clipboard for my clerical test: 40 questions about alphabetizing. After I completed it, she told me, "Your interview will be in just a minute." A black woman came in. She was nervous. She wore a red shiny dress with geranium perfume. She wanted a clerical job too. The receptionist told her she needed at least two years' experience for clerical work. So the woman in red left and a minute later I was called in to another room. The interview lasted thirty seconds and ended with, "Give us a call between 4 o'clock and 4:30 tomorrow and we'll see if there are any jobs for you."

Like a telephone home

We came across a land
of soft felt hats
with the wind ironed flat
and worn like a uniform

The other apartment sounds like a penguin nesting ground.

My change at the market is $19.09.
I go outside thinking about that year.

F Train to Broadway:
"Would you marry my daughter?"
"I would *never* marry your whore daughter!"

Looking for a job in the sarcophagus,
questioned by a 2,000 year old mummy with
a paunch.

D Train to Brooklyn:
"You can kiss my ass!"
"You got a husband? You ask *him* to do that!"

When I answered the door, a man and a woman stood there. "We're neighbors of yours," he began, "And as neighbors, we all feel the right to defend against one of the biggest enemies of our day." I was frozen like an eggbeater. "Do you think it will ever be possible for us to leave our doors unlocked?" Before I could answer, he said, "Tell me, do you believe in the Good Lord Jesus Christ when he says I will make it so you don't have to lock your doors anymore?" I have to admit I started to smile, and he almost did too, but then he continued, "We're going to all our neighbors today and giving them this message of Peace." Now he was serious with capital letters. "I have a couple booklets with me. I'd like to give you one, or both of these. For a minimal charge of a quarter or whatever you have." They were both made of gingerbread. "I'm sorry," I stumbled, "I have to go, really I have to go to work now," even though it was 12, as I pointed over towards Coney Island. My mind was on steel tracks then hurtling down and around with roller coaster speed. "Oh!" he said, startled, as if the oven was set too high and the gingerbread couple was pounding on the door with hardening fists, "Well here, please take this." He handed me a booklet called *Life in a Peaceful New World*. Children played on panda bears. Lions watched over them. Trees, a blue sky and a mountain in the distance. You could walk into that world and it was calm as a museum painting.

✳

The cockroaches flamenco when the lights go out.

She came quietly across the fine line of dreaming into this reality and she was smiling more
times around than her scarf. I can swear I'll be
happy again.

Under the painting of a man with no pants.

So glad to see
her fingers again

Better stop writing about her...
or we'll wind up with another
NOVEL

Something I forgot to mention:
in the subway a few days ago
I saw Alice in Wonderland

Feb 25, 1989

Only a girl would notice you bite your finger-
nails.

Lost in the subways after falling down from
that, going back and forth underground, wast-
ing hours trying to find the way home.

Feb 26, 1989

At least we have Louis Armstrong

Her room was the warmest I've ever been in
like an invisible circus around us

Feb 27, 1989

Just noticed she thinks of me
(2 days too late) Sorry.

Someone on the subway reading a comic book
says aloud, "Oh, I forgot. You control the mood
I'm in."

Feb 28, 1989

The American Polygraph Association
"Dedicated to Truth" seems to be just
another way of trapping you in a room
with wax McCarthy's ghost asking you
questions like, "How do you rate your
honesty?" and after all was said and done
I walked out with their pen.

Pulling March on like a discount sweater
racked between winter and spring

Going up in the elevator with me is a man who
saw Ella Fitzgerald sing at the Apollo. He is trying to impress the woman next to him. When
the doors open and she leaves on the 3rd floor,
he calls after her, "Don't you know who Chick
Webb is?" I say I do, but he doesn't answer. I
can't believe after all these years he's still using
this as a pickup line, never knowing it's become
a mothballed movie theater.

Someone digging sand traps next door

That hurt like a Renaissance toothache

In Central Park today, escaping from the office for the green wind of park statues and pigeons, I was eating a cheese sandwich under the singing trees and I heard a cry for help. When I got up to investigate, the voice seemed further away, like leaving, so I almost tripped over him in my hurry. When I discovered him he was the size of a cola bottle. He was shrinking away fast, yelling out little lungs. There was nothing I could do (thinking maybe I could cup my hands about him like a carbonated matchstick) but I could only watch him shrink into a cigarette signature and blow away like the smallest wind-up biplane toy.

Mar 4-5, 1989

How could I forget about gravity?

Mar 6, 1989

Like a thousand bees paying homage to a painting of fruit

Mar 7, 1989

His land was greener than any park. The birds would fly to him instead. They could get over the tall fence. Sometimes commuters would see him on the other side, riding a white horse. All around him the skyscrapers towered like bad tempers. They tried to hold back the sunlight but it slipped in anyway, making pastures glow like neon.

Mar 8, 1989

Beautifully pirate-shipped with galoshes

She is closer to Coney Island

They are

very much

Astronomers

in

America

I bought her a quart of Florida orange juice.

Fish will never visit the moon

The Great Zorbina thought of all the cats in New York windows, waiting out the day for someone to come home.

Mar 10, 1989

The train stopped so suddenly she fell onto the floor. Everyone around her helped her to stand.

Mar 11, 1989

Like the lost things of childhood
painted so bright and wooden
ending up who knows where

Rolling the words:
West Coast
Seattle

Mar 12, 1989

He would have to admit defeat
like a Confederate gentleman
handing over his sword

*My landlord Yuko and her boyfriend were doppelgangers of Yoko Ono and John Lennon and enjoyed playing the part. But I'm quite sure she was perplexed by my late-rent note, signing off as "The Tenant of the Baskervilles."

Mar 13, 1989

Humanous, the luminous human, so bright he turns his friends into shadows on the floor, turns people and things into instant candle wax—a door will melt into butter as he enters and the room will become an instant sea of colors, spilled out like a pack of crayons. Poor Humanous hasn't talked to anyone in burned away calendar months—not since he stood at the edge of the Grand Canyon and shouted across to somebody who would answer him moments later. But it may have been just an echo.

Mar 14, 1989

The milkman's daughter watched him leave in the cold early morning. Across the sidewalks and over rooftops, delivering the moon measured into bottles.

Mar 15, 1989

The last century, lying on the floor

Mar 16. 1989

The last Passenger Pigeon, dwindled down from millions, whittled into this one moth-eaten bird, stuffed, trapped in glass, sitting for photographs from now on. Before it died, it didn't even know its mirror image—thinking there's another one just like me!

She led her child through the museum, window to window, telling him, "That's a boy monkey. That's a girl monkey," using monkeys to explain the birds and the bees.

Mar 17, 1989

When I was born, America was a different America. Geronimo was still alive.

I remember Sally's white stockings. Now the sad thing is, I wonder what we talked about. I'd like to know. Pets and animals were always on my list. My black dog who chased rocks in the backyard. I surrounded myself with dinosaurs and got an allowance on Saturday. Imagination constantly. I was living forever in the time I had then.

Mar 18, 1989

A movie theater where all the old people come to remember their favorite Hollywood gods. They glow from the screen and reach far back into the shadows.

Returned to the library, looking for her last name in the phone book, hoping her number will land on my hand.

Mar 19, 1989

A tomato from the bodega

Mar 20-23, 1989

The Magnificent Marvelous Magic Man says he can play every instrument in the world, but he chooses a comb and a piece of torn newspaper. He plays the "Hawaii 5-0" theme twice.

"Why is tomorrow a holiday?"

"It's Good Friday! What are you? You're not Catholic, or Christian, or—"

"No."

"Oh—you're a heathen!"

"Okay," I said.

"Well, don't let the boss hear you say that. He's a Christian."

"Thanks for the warning."

"You're one of those scientist types, aren't you?"

"What?"

"You believe people come from monkeys and apes."

I saw two people so angry they pretended to
shoot guns at each other.

Mar 24, 1989

Alexander Graham Bell's Frankenstein is
a bill for $117 from New York Telephone

Once upon a time, my father cooked macaroni
in the Arctic.

WHEN YOU SMILE YOU LET IN LIGHT

Written by Allen Frost 1988-1989

Books by Good Deed Rain

Saint Lemonade, Allen Frost, 2014. Two novels illustrated by the author in the manner of the old Big Little Books.

Playground, Allen Frost, 2014. Poems collected from seven years of chapbooks.

Roosevelt, Allen Frost, 2015. A Pacific Northwest novel set in July, 1942, when a boy and a girl search for a missing elephant. Illustrated throughout by Fred Sodt.

5 Novels, Allen Frost, 2015. Novels written over five years, featuring circus giants, clockwork animals, detectives and time travelers.

The Sylvan Moore Show, Allen Frost, 2015. A short story omnibus of 193 stories written over 30 years.

Town in a Cloud, Allen Frost, 2015. A 3 part book of poetry, written during the Bellingham rainy seasons of fall, winter, and spring.

A Flutter of Birds Passing Through Heaven: A Tribute to Robert Sund. 2016. Edited by Allen Frost and Paul Piper. The story of a legendary Ish River poet & artist.

At the Edge of America, Allen Frost, 2016. Two novels in one book blend time travel in a mythical poetic America.

Lake Erie Submarine, Allen Frost, 2016. A two week vacation in Ohio inspired these poems, illustrated by the author.

and Light, Paul Piper, 2016. Poetry written over three years. Illustrated with watercolors by Penny Piper.

The Book of Ticks, Allen Frost, 2017. A giant collection of 8 mysterious adventures featuring Phil Ticks. Illustrated throughout by Aaron Gunderson.

I Can Only Imagine, Allen Frost, 2017. Five adventures of love and heartbreak dreamed in an imaginary world. Cover & color illustrations by Annabelle Barrett.

The Orphanage of Abandoned Teenagers, Allen Frost, 2017. A fictional guide for teens and their parents. Illustrated by the author.

In the Valley of Mystic Light: An Oral History of the Skagit Valley Arts Scene, 2017. Edited by Claire Swedberg & Rita Hupy.

Different Planet, Allen Frost, 2017. Four science fiction adventures: reincarnation, robots, talking animals, outer space and clones. Cover & illustrations by Laura Vasyutynska.

Go with the Flow: A Tribute to Clyde Sanborn. 2018. Edited by Allen Frost. The life and art of a timeless river poet.

Homeless Sutra, Allen Frost, 2018. Four stories: Sylvan Moore, a flying monk, a water salesman, and a guardian rabbit.

The Lake Walker, Allen Frost 2018. A little novel set in black and white like one of those old European movies about death and life.

A Hundred Dreams Ago, Allen Frost, 2018. A winter book of poetry and prose. Illustrated by Aaron Gunderson.

Almost Animals, Allen Frost, 2018. A collection of linked stories, thinking about what makes us animals.

The Robotic Age, Allen Frost, 2018. A vaudeville magician and his robot track down ghosts. Illustrated throughout by Aaron Gunderson.

Kennedy, Allen Frost, 2018. This sequel to Roosevelt is a coming-of-age fable set during two weeks in 1962 in a mythical Kennedy-land. Illustrated throughout by Fred Sodt.

Fable, Allen Frost, 2018. There's something going on in this country and I can best relate it in fable: the parable of the rabbits, a bedtime story, and the diary of our trip to Ohio.

Elbows & Knees: Essays & Plays, Allen Frost, 2018. A thrilling collection of writing about some of my favorite subjects, from B-movies to Brautigan.

The Last Paper Stars, Allen Frost 2019. A trip back in time to the 20 year old mind of Frankenstein, and two other worlds of the future.

Walt Amherst is Awake, Allen Frost, 2019. The dreamlife of an office worker. Illustrated throughout by Aaron Gunderson.

When You Smile You Let in Light, Allen Frost, 2019. An atomic love story written by a 23 year old.

YUKO I COULDN'T
     GET MY CHECK
FOR TODAY — I'LL
TRY TOMORROW, IF NOT THEN
TUESDAY IS AS SOON AS I CAN

— The tenant of the Baskervilles